KT-422-266

Scenes of Academic Life

Selected from his novels by

DAVID LODGE

PENGUIN BOOKS

PENGUIN BOOKS

Published by the Penguin Group
Penguin Books Ltd, 80 Strand, London WC2R ORL, England
Penguin Group (USA) Inc., 375 Hudson Street, New York, New York 10014, USA
Penguin Group (Canada), 10 Alcorn Avenue, Toronto, Ontario, Canada M4V 3B2
(a division of Pearson Penguin Canada Inc.)
Penguin Ireland, 25 St Stephen's Green, Dublin 2, Ireland
(a division of Penguin Books Ltd)
Penguin Group (Australia), 250 Camberwell Road, Camberwell, Victoria 3124,
Australia (a division of Pearson Australia Group Pty Ltd)
Penguin Books India Pvt Ltd, 11 Community Centre,
Panchsheel Park, New Delhi – 110 017, India
Penguin Group (NZ), cnr Airborne and Rosedale Roads, Albany,
Auckland 1310, New Zealand (a division of Pearson New Zealand Ltd)
Penguin Books (South Africa) (Pty) Ltd, 24 Sturdee Avenue,
Rosebank 2196, South Africa

Penguin Books Ltd, Registered Offices: 80 Strand, London WC2R ORL, England

www.penguin.com

'It Looked Like Snow' from *The British Museum is Falling
Down*, first published by MacGibbon & Kee 1965
Published in Penguin Books 1983
'Two Types of Academic' from *Changing Places*, first published by
Martin Secker & Warburg Ltd 1975
Published in Penguin Books 1978
'Textuality as Striptease' and '*wheeeeeeeeeeeeeeeeeEEEEEEEEEEEEE!*' from
Small World, first published by Martin Secker & Warburg Ltd 1984
Published in Penguin Books 1985
'Just a Cigarette' and 'A Tutorial' from *Nice Work*, first published by
Martin Secker & Warburg Ltd 1988
Published in Penguin Books 1989
This selection published as a Pocket Penguin 2005

1

Copyright © David Lodge, 1965, 1975, 1984, 1988, 2005
All rights reserved

The moral right of the author has been asserted

Set in 11/13pt Monotype Dante
Typeset by Palimpsest Book Production Limited
Polmont, Stirlingshire
Printed in England by Clays Ltd, St Ives plc

In
1935 if you wanted to
read a good book, you needed
either a lot of money or a library card.
Cheap paperbacks were available, but their
poor production generally mirrored the quality
between the covers. One weekend that year,
Allen Lane, Managing Director of The Bodley Head,
having spent the weekend visiting Agatha Christie,
found himself on a platform at Exeter station trying to
find something to read for his journey back to London.
He was appalled by the quality of the material he had to
choose from. Everything that Allen Lane achieved from that
day until his death in 1970 was based on a passionate belief
in the existence of 'a vast reading public for *intelligent*
books at a low price'. The result of his momentous vision
was the birth not only of Penguin, but of the 'paperback
revolution'. Quality writing became available for the price of
a packet of cigarettes, literature became a mass medium
for the first time, a nation of book-borrowers became a
nation of book-buyers – and the very concept of book
publishing was changed for ever. Those founding
principles – of quality and value, with an overarching
belief in the fundamental importance of reading –
have guided everything the company has
done since 1935. Sir Allen Lane's
pioneering spirit is still very much alive
at Penguin in 2005. Here's to
the next 70 years!

MORE THAN A BUSINESS

'We decided it was time to end the almost customary half-hearted manner in which cheap editions were produced – as though the only people who could possibly want cheap editions must belong to a lower order of intelligence. We, however, believed in the existence in this country of a vast reading public for intelligent books at a low price, and staked everything on it'
Sir Allen Lane, 1902–1970

'The Penguin Books are splendid value for sixpence, so splendid that if other publishers had any sense they would combine against them and suppress them'
George Orwell

'More than a business … a national cultural asset'
Guardian

'When you look at the whole Penguin achievement you know that it constitutes, in action, one of the more democratic successes of our recent social history'
Richard Hoggart

Contents

Foreword

This little book contains a personal selection of scenes from my novels of academic life, sometimes called 'campus novels', though the word 'campus' was relatively new in Britain when the first of them, *The British Museum is Falling Down*, was published in 1965. 'Campus' was of course originally an American usage (of the Latin word for 'field'), and the campus novel was also an American invention. Mary McCarthy's *The Groves of Academe* (1952), a satirical story of political and personal intrigues among the faculty at a liberal arts college, has a claim to be the first of its kind, and the literary-pastoral associations of the title are relevant to most subsequent examples of the genre in both England and America, even when their physical location is a civic redbrick institution, as in the seminal English campus novel, Kingsley Amis's *Lucky Jim* (1954). The campus novel is typically focused on the humanities rather than the sciences, and treats the university as a piece of territory somewhat removed from the hurly-burly of ordinary life, a 'small world' in which ambition and desire generate comedy rather than tragedy. There is invariably an element of artifice and literary self-consciousness in the genre, of which Shakespeare's courtly campus play, *Love's Labour's Lost*, was a distant precursor.

Nevertheless the campus novel has reflected real

changes both in academic culture and in society at large over the last fifty-odd years, and in revisiting my own books to make this selection I am struck by the extent of the mutations. *Changing Places*, for instance, set in 1969, now seems like a historical novel, and may soon need annotation to be completely comprehensible to younger readers. Its comedy is largely based on differences between academic life in England and in America, many of which no longer obtain. The two systems have drawn closer together: American universities have become less euphoric places, English universities more competitive, as have the countries to which they belong. The massive expansion of British higher education, Thatcherite economics, and the hegemony of 'management' in every sector of society, have forced our universities to adopt American-style modular courses, largely abandon traditional tutorial teaching, and purge their faculties of the amusing unproductive eccentrics who once found a comfortable home there. The action of *Small World* takes place in 1979, the year Mrs Thatcher was elected to power. International conference-going would never be so easy or so exciting again, certainly for British academics: travel grants became much more difficult to get subsequently, and the prime object of going to a conference was to add another line to your CV rather than to enlarge your horizons. The tutorial system still survives at Rummidge University in *Nice Work*, set in 1986 and published two years later, but its days were numbered; and in other respects the novel presents a picture of university life that will be recognizable to present-day students and teachers, one in which the pastoral seclusion of the campus, whether literal or metaphorical, from the real world of social, political and economic forces, has gone for ever. Yet it was over this very same period that many of the best and brightest minds in the humanities, as if in some instinctive, collective act of resistance to the new climate of pragmatism and accountability in higher education, embraced a system of thought, loosely known as Theory, which subverted common sense and was almost incomprehensible to the layman. This phenomenon is also represented in these pages.

David Lodge, 2005

It Looked Like Snow

Adam Appleby is a postgraduate student at the University of London in the early 1960s, researching and writing a thesis on the modern English novel in the Round Reading Room of the British Museum, where the British Library was then situated. He is a practising Catholic and married to one. This couple's efforts to obey the Church's teaching on birth control by means of the 'rhythm method', or periodic abstinence, have so far resulted in three children in four years; and on the day of the novel's action Adam has reason to fear that Barbara may be pregnant again. Under the stress of this anxiety Adam is subject to hallucinations in which his experience comes to him transformed by the characteristic styles of various modern novelists. In this passage a visit to his supervisor is reported in a manner that parodies C. P. Snow's novels about the political and personal intrigues of ambitious scientists, civil servants and Cambridge dons (never observed doing any teaching) in what he called 'the corridors of power'. The novels are narrated by a character called Lewis Eliot in a style prone to banality and redundancy.

It was cold and damp on the pavement outside Student Christian Hall. The leafless trees in Gordon Square stood black and gaunt against the façade of Georgian houses. The sky was cold and grey. It looked like snow.

4

I hunched my shoulders inside my coat and set off briskly in the direction of the English department (*Adam Appleby might have written*). I had an appointment with Briggs, my supervisor. He was a punctual man, and appreciated punctuality in others. I mean that he liked people to be on time. Men who have sacrificed a lot of big things to their careers often cling fiercely to small habits.

Access to the English Department was through a small courtyard at the rear of the College. There seemed to be a lot of young people about, and I had to linger some moments before I caught the eye of Jones, the Beadle. I always make a point of catching the eye of beadles, porters and similar servants. Jones did not disappoint me: his face lit up.

'Hallo, sir. Haven't seen you for some time.'

'Come to see Mr Briggs, Jones. There seem to be a lot of people about?'

'Undergraduates, sir,' he explained.

The English Department wasn't the most distinguished building in the College, but it had history. The brick façade, stained with soot and streaked with rain water, was thought to be a good example of its type, which was turn-of-the-century warehousing. When, some thirty years ago, the expanding College had bought the freehold, rather than demolish the building they had skilfully converted the interior into classrooms and narrow, cell-like offices by means of matchboard partitions. It wasn't what you could call a comfortable or elegant building, but it had character. Its small, grimy windows looked on to an identical building twenty feet away, which housed the

Department of Civil Engineering. But, schooled by long practice, I turned into the right door and mounted the long stone staircase.

The door of Briggs' room on the second floor was open, and the sound of conversation floated into the corridor. I tapped on the door and extended my head into the room.

'Oh, come in, Appleby,' said Briggs.

He was talking to Bane, who had recently been appointed to a new Chair of Absurdist Drama, endowed by a commercial television company. This, I knew, had been a blow to Briggs, who was the senior man of the two, and who had been looking about for a Chair for some time. His own field was the English Essay. No one was likely to endow a special Chair in the English Essay, and Briggs knew it. His best chance of promotion lay in the retirement of the Head of Department, old Howells, who was always raising Briggs's expectations by retreating at the beginning of term to a Swiss sanatorium, only to dash them again by returning refreshed and reinvigorated at the beginning of the vacations.

The posture of the two men seemed to illustrate their relationship. Bane was sprawled in Briggs's lumpy armchair, his legs stretched out over the brown linoleum. Briggs stood by the window, uneasily fingering the ridges of the radiator. On his desk was an open bottle of British sherry. At my appearance he seemed to straighten up his tired, slack body, and to become his usual efficient, slightly fussy self.

'Come in, come in,' he repeated.

'I don't want to interrupt you . . .'

'No, come in. You know Professor Bane, of course?'

Bane nodded casually, but affably enough. 'How's the research going?' he asked.

'I hope to start writing soon,' I replied.

'Will you take a glass of sherry wine?' said Briggs, who affected such redundancies in his speech.

'Thank you, but I've already lunched,' I explained.

Briggs glanced at his watch. 'I suppose it *is* late. What does your wrist-watch say, Bane?'

'A quarter to two.'

'We've been talking, and forgot the time,' said Briggs. If Briggs was losing his habit of punctuality, I thought, he must be seriously affected by the promotion of Bane.

Bane got up and stretched himself nonchalantly. 'Well, I think we've talked it out now,' he said. 'Perhaps you'll think it over, Briggs, and let me know what you decide.'

Briggs bit his lip, at the same time pulling nervously on the lobes of both ears. It was a little nervous habit of his which you didn't notice at first.

'I must say,' he said, 'it surprises me a little that the Prof hasn't mentioned this to me at all.'

Bane shrugged. 'Of course, you realize that it means nothing to me, and the last thing I want to do is to put you to any inconvenience. But it seems that the Prof wants all the people with Chairs' – he leaned slightly on the word – 'together on one floor. I think you'll find my little room on the fourth floor quite snug. At least one doesn't suffer from interruptions up there. Put it this way: you'll be able to get on with your book,' he concluded maliciously. Briggs had been working for twenty years on a history of the English Essay.

As Briggs opened his mouth to reply, he was forestalled by a frenzied crashing in the radiator pipes, emanating from the boilers far below, but filling the room with such a din as to render speech inaudible. While the racket continued, the three of us stood, motionless and silent, lost in our own thoughts. I felt a certain thrill at being witness to one of those classic struggles for power and prestige which characterize the lives of ambitious men and which, in truth, exhaust most of their time and energy. To the casual observer, it might seem that nothing important was at stake here, but it might well be that the future course of English studies in the University hung upon this conversation.

At length the noise in the radiator pipes diminished, and faded away. Briggs said:

'I'm glad you mentioned my book, Bane. To be honest with you, the thing I have most against a move is my collection here.' Briggs gestured towards the huge, ugly, worm-eaten bookcase that housed his collection of the English essayists: Addison, Steele, Johnson, Lamb, Hazlitt, Belloc, Chesterton . . . even Egbert Merrymarsh was represented here by a slim, white-buckram volume privately printed by Carthusian monks on hand-made paper. 'I just don't see how it will fit into your room,' explained Briggs.

This was Briggs' trump-card. His collection was famous, and no one would dare to suggest that he break it up. Bane lost his nonchalant air, and looked cross: a faint flush coloured his pouchy cheeks. 'I'll get Jones to

8

take some measurements,' he said abruptly, and left the room.

Briggs brightened momentarily at Bane's departure, no doubt consoled by the thought that Jones was in his own pocket. But the hidden pressures of the discussion had taken their toll, and he seemed a tired and defeated man as he sank into his desk-chair.

'Well,' he said at length, 'how's the research going?'

'I hope to start writing soon,' I replied. 'But I fear I won't be able to submit in June. I think I'll have to get an extension to October.'

'That's a pity, Appleby, a great pity. I disapprove of theses running on and on. Look at Camel, for instance.'

'Yes, I know. What worries me is the question of jobs. I really will need a job next academic year.'

'A job? A university post, is it that you want, Appleby?'

'Yes, I –'

I was about to allude delicately to the possibility of a vacancy in the Department, caused by Bane's new Chair, when Briggs went on, with startling emphasis:

'Then I have only one word of advice to you, Appleby. Publish! Publish or perish! That's how it is in the academic world these days. There was a time when appointments were made on a more human basis, but not any more.'

'The snag is, nothing I have is quite ready for publication . . .'

With an effort, Briggs dragged his attention away from his private discontents and brought it to bear on mine. But the energy went out of his voice, and he seemed bored.

'What about that piece you showed me on Merrymarsh?' he said vaguely.

'Do you really think . . . It's my impression there's not much interest in Merrymarsh these days.'

'Interest? Interest doesn't matter, as long as you get it published. Who do you suppose is interested in Absurdist drama?'

I left Briggs staring moodily into his empty sherry-glass. On my way out of the building I met Bane again, and took the opportunity to ask his advice on a trivial bibliographical problem. He seemed flattered by the enquiry, and took me up to his room to look up the reference.

When I finally made my departure, the trees were still there in Gordon Square, bleak and gaunt against the Georgian façade. I walked back to the Museum under a cold grey sky. I wondered idly which man I disliked most, Briggs or Bane.

Two Types of Academic

Changing Places: a tale of two campuses begins on the first day of 1969, with two forty-year-old professors of English Literature – Philip Swallow, who is actually only a Lecturer at the University of Rummidge in the English Midlands, and Morris Zapp of Euphoric State University on the West Coast of America – passing each other in airplanes above the polar icecap, *en route* to exchange jobs for six months. For Philip it is a welcome break from domestic and professional routine; for Morris a temporary solution to a marital crisis. Usually, the narrator observes, only the cream of the academic staff at Rummidge enjoyed the privilege of taking part in this exchange scheme between the two universities, while Euphoric State often had difficulty in persuading any of its faculty to go to grimy, provincial Rummidge . . .

The exchange of Philip Swallow and Morris Zapp, however, constituted a reversal of the usual pattern. Zapp was distinguished, and Swallow was not. Zapp was the man who had published articles in *PMLA* while still in graduate school; who, enviably offered his first job by Euphoric State, had stuck out for twice the going salary, and got it; who had published five fiendishly clever books (four of them on Jane Austen) by the time he was thirty and achieved the rank of full professor at the same precocious age. Swallow was a man scarcely known outside his own Department, who had published nothing except a handful of essays and reviews, who had risen slowly up the salary scale of Lecturer by standard annual increments and was now halted at the top with slender prospects of promotion. Not that Philip Swallow was lacking in intelligence or ability; but he lacked will and ambition, the professional killer instinct which Zapp abundantly possessed.

In this respect both men were characteristic of the educational systems they had passed through. In America, it is not too difficult to obtain a bachelor's degree. The student is left very much to his own devices, he accumulates the necessary credits at his leisure, cheating is easy, and there is not much suspense or anxiety about the eventual outcome. He (or she) is therefore free to give full attention to the normal interests of late adolescence – sport, alcohol, entertainment and the opposite sex. It is at the postgraduate level that the pressure really begins, when the student is burnished and tempered in a series of gruelling courses and rigorous assessments until he is deemed worthy to receive the accolade of the PhD. By now he has invested so much time and money in the process that any career other than an academic one has become unthinkable, and anything less than success in it unbearable. He is well primed, in short, to enter a profession as steeped in the spirit of free enterprise as Wall Street, in which each scholar-teacher makes an individual contract with his employer, and is free to sell his services to the highest bidder.

Under the British system, competition begins and ends much earlier. Four times, under our educational rules, the human pack is shuffled and cut – at eleven-plus, sixteen-plus, eighteen-plus and twenty-plus – and happy is he who comes top of the deck on each occasion, but especially the last. This is called Finals, the very name of which implies that nothing of importance can happen after it. The British postgraduate student is a lonely, forlorn soul, uncertain of what he is doing or whom he is trying to please – you may recognize him in the tea-shops around the Bodleian and the British Museum by the glazed look in his eyes, the vacant stare of the shell-shocked veteran for whom nothing has been real since the Big Push. As long as he manages to land his first job, this is no great handicap in the short run, since tenure is virtually automatic in British universities, and everyone is paid on the same scale. But at a certain age, the age at which promotion and Chairs begin to occupy a man's thoughts, he may look back with wistful nostalgia to the days when his wits ran fresh and clear, directed to a single, positive goal.

Philip Swallow had been made and unmade by the system in precisely this way. He liked examinations, always did well in them. Finals had been, in many ways, the supreme moment of his life. He frequently dreamed that he was taking the examinations again, and these were happy dreams. Awake, he could without difficulty remember the questions he had elected to answer on every paper that hot, distant June. In the preceding months he had prepared himself with meticulous care, filling his mind with distilled knowledge, drop by drop, until, on the eve of the first paper (Old English Set Texts), it was almost brimming over. Each morning for the next ten days he bore this precious vessel to the examination halls and poured a measured quantity of the contents onto pages of ruled quarto. Day by day the level fell, until on the tenth day the vessel was empty, the cup was drained, the cupboard was bare. In the years that followed he set about replenishing his mind, but it was never quite the same. The sense of purpose was lacking – there was no great Reckoning against which he could hoard his knowledge, so that it tended to leak away as fast as he acquired it.

Philip Swallow was a man with a genuine love of literature in all its diverse forms. He was as happy with *Beowulf* as with Virginia Woolf, with *Waiting for Godot* as with *Gammer Gurton's Needle*, and in odd moments when nobler examples of the written word were not to hand he read attentively the backs of cornflakes packets, the small print on railway tickets and the advertising matter in books of stamps. This undiscriminating enthusiasm, however, prevented him from settling on a 'field' to cultivate as his own. He had done his initial research on Jane Austen, but since then had turned his attention to topics as various as medieval sermons, Elizabethan sonnet sequences, Restoration heroic tragedy, eighteenth-century broadsides, the novels of William Godwin, the poetry of Elizabeth Barrett Browning and premonitions of the Theatre of the Absurd in the plays of George Bernard Shaw. None of these projects had been completed. Seldom, indeed, had he drawn up a preliminary bibliography before his attention was distracted by some new or revived interest in something entirely different. He ran hither and thither between the shelves of Eng. Lit. like a child in a toyshop – so reluctant to choose one item to the exclusion of others that he ended up empty-handed.

There was one respect alone in which Philip was recognized as a man of distinction, though only within the confines of his own Department. He was a superlative examiner of undergraduates: scrupulous, painstaking, stern yet just. No one could award a delicate mark like B+/B+?+ with such confident aim, or justify it with such cogency and conviction. In the Department meetings that discussed draft question papers he was much feared by his colleagues because of his keen eye for the ambiguous rubric, the repetition of questions from previous years' papers, the careless oversight that would allow candidates to duplicate material in two answers. His own papers were works of art on which he laboured with loving care for many hours, tinkering and polishing, weighing every word, deftly manipulating *either*s and *or*s, judiciously balancing difficult questions on popular authors with easy questions on obscure ones, inviting candidates to consider, illustrate, comment on, analyse, respond to, make discriminating assessments of or (last resort) discuss brilliant epigrams of his own invention disguised as quotations from anonymous critics.

A colleague had once declared that Philip ought to publish his examination papers. The suggestion had been intended as a sneer, but Philip had been rather taken with the idea – seeing in it, for a few dizzy hours, a heaven-sent solution to his professional barrenness. He visualized a critical work of totally revolutionary form, a concise, comprehensive survey of English literature consisting entirely of questions, elegantly printed with acres of white paper between them, questions that would be miracles of condensation, eloquence and thoughtfulness, questions to read and re-read, questions to brood over, as pregnant and enigmatic as *haikus*, as memorable as proverbs; questions that would, so to speak, contain within themselves the ghostly, subtly suggested embryos of their own answers. *Collected Literary Questions*, by Philip Swallow. A book to be compared with Pascal's *Pensées* or Wittgenstein's *Philosophical Investigations* . . .

But the project had advanced no further than his more orthodox ones, and meanwhile the Rummidge students had begun agitating for the abolition of conventional examinations, so that his one special skill was in danger of becoming redundant. There had been times, lately, when he had begun to wonder whether he was entirely suited to the career on which he had been launched some fifteen years earlier, not so much by personal choice as by the mere impetus of his remarkable First.

For years Morris Zapp had, like a man exceptionally blessed with good health, taken his self-confidence for granted, and regarded the recurrent identity crises of his colleagues as symptoms of psychic hypochondria. But recently he had caught himself brooding about the meaning of his life, no less. This was partly the consequence of his own success. He was full professor at one of the most prestigious and desirably located universities in America, and had already served as the Chairman of his Department for three years under Euphoric State's rotating system; he was a highly respected scholar with a long and impressive list of publications to his name. He could only significantly increase his salary either by moving to some god-awful place in Texas or the Mid-West where no one in his right mind would go for a thousand dollars a day, or by switching to administration, looking for a college President's job somewhere, which in the present state of the nation's campuses was a through ticket to an early grave. At the age of forty, in short, Morris Zapp could think of nothing he wanted to achieve that he hadn't achieved already, and this depressed him.

There was always his research, of course, but some of the zest had gone out of that since it ceased to be a means to an end. He couldn't enhance his reputation, he could only damage it, by adding further items to his bibliography, and the realization slowed him down, made him cautious. Some years ago he had embarked with great enthusiasm on an ambitious critical project: a series of commentaries on Jane Austen which would work through the whole canon, one novel at a time, saying absolutely everything that could possibly be said about them. The idea was to be utterly exhaustive, to examine the novels from every conceivable angle, historical, biographical, rhetorical, mythical, Freudian, Jungian, existentialist, Marxist, structuralist, Christian-allegorical, ethical, exponential, linguistic, phenomenological, archetypal, you name it; so that when each commentary was written there would be simply *nothing further to say* about the novel in question. The object of the exercise, as he had often to explain with as much patience as he could muster, was not to enhance others' enjoyment and understanding of Jane Austen, still less to honour the novelist herself, but to put a definitive stop to the production of any further garbage on the subject. The commentaries would not be designed for the general reader but for the specialist, who, looking up Zapp, would find that the book, article or thesis he had been planning had already been anticipated and, more likely than not, invalidated. After Zapp, the rest would be silence. The thought gave him deep satisfaction. In Faustian moments he dreamed of going on, after fixing Jane Austen, to do the same job on the other major English novelists, then the poets and dramatists, perhaps using computers and teams of trained graduate students, inexorably reducing the area of English literature available for free comment, spreading dismay through the whole industry, rendering scores of his colleagues redundant: periodicals would fall silent, famous English Departments be left deserted like ghost towns . . .

As is perhaps obvious, Morris Zapp had no great esteem for his fellow-labourers in the vineyards of literature. They seemed to him vague, fickle, irresponsible creatures, who wallowed in relativism like hippopotami in mud, with their nostrils barely protruding into the air of common-sense. They happily tolerated the existence of opinions contrary to their own – they even, for God's sake, sometimes changed their minds. Their pathetic attempts at profundity were qualified out of existence and largely interrogative in mode. They liked to begin a paper with some formula like, 'I want to raise some questions about so-and-so', and seemed to think they had done their intellectual duty by merely raising them. This manoeuvre drove Morris Zapp insane. Any damn fool, he maintained, could think of questions; it was *answers* that separated the men from the boys. If you couldn't answer your own questions it was either because you hadn't worked on them hard enough or because they weren't real questions. In either case you should keep your mouth shut. One couldn't move in English studies these days without falling over unanswered questions which some damn fool had carelessly left lying about – it was like trying to mend a leak in an attic full of dusty, broken furniture. Well, his commentary would put a stop to that, at least as far as Jane Austen was concerned.

But the work proceeded slowly; he was not yet halfway through *Sense and Sensibility* and already it was obvious that each commentary would run to several volumes. Apart from the occasional article, he hadn't published anything for several years now. Sometimes he would start work on a problem only to remember, after some hours' cogitation, that he had solved it very satisfactorily himself years before. Over the same period – whether as cause or effect he wasn't sure – he had begun to feel ill-at-ease in his own body. He was prone to indigestion after rich restaurant meals, he usually needed a sleeping-pill before retiring, he was developing a pot-belly, and he found it increasingly difficult to achieve more than one orgasm in a single session – or so he would complain to his buddies over a beer. The truth was that these days he couldn't count on making it even once, and Désirée had less cause for resentment than she knew over the baby-sitter last summer. Things weren't what they used to be in the Zapp loins, though it was a dark truth that he would scarcely admit to himself, let alone to anyone else. He would not publicly acknowledge, either, that he was finding it a strain to hold his students' attention as the climate on campus became increasingly hostile to traditional academic values. His style of teaching was designed to shock conventionally educated students out of a sloppily reverent attitude to literature and into an ice-cool, intellectually rigorous one. It could do little with students openly contemptuous of both the subject and his own qualifications. His barbed wisecracks sank harmlessly into the protective padding of the new gentle inarticulacy, which had become so fashionable that even his brightest graduate students, ruthless professionals at heart, felt obliged to conform to it, mumbling in seminars, 'Well, it's like James, ah, well the guy *wants* to be a modern, I mean he has the symbolism bit and God is dead and all, but it's like he's still committed to intelligence, like he thinks it all *means* something for Chrissake – you dig?' Jane Austen was certainly not the writer to win the hearts of the new generation. Sometimes Morris woke sweating from nightmares in which students paraded round the campus carrying placards that declared KNIGHTLEY SUCKS and FANNY PRICE IS A FINK. Perhaps he *was* getting a little stale; perhaps, after all, he would profit from a change of scene.

In this fashion had Morris Zapp rationalized the decision forced upon him by Désirée's ultimatum. But, sitting in the airplane beside pregnant Mary Makepeace, all these reasons seemed unconvincing. If he needed a change, he was fairly sure it wasn't the kind that England would afford. He had neither affection nor respect for the British. The ones he had met – expatriates and visiting professors – mostly acted like fags and then turned out not to be, which he found unsettling. At parties they wolfed your canapés and gulped your gin as if they had just been released from prison, and talked all the time in high, twittering voices about the differences between the English and American university systems, making it clear that they regarded the latter as a huge, rather amusing racket from which they were personally determined to take the biggest possible cut in the shortest possible time. Their publications were vapid and amateurish, inadequately researched, slackly argued, and riddled with so many errors, misquotations, misattributions and incorrect dates that it was amazing they managed to get their own names right on the title page. They nevertheless had the nerve to treat American scholars, including even himself, with sneering condescension in their lousy journals.

He felt in his bones that he wasn't going to enjoy England: he would be lonely and bored, all the more so because he had taken a small provisional vow not to be unfaithful to Désirée, just to annoy her; and it was the worst possible place to carry on his research. Once he sank into the bottomless morass of English manners, he would never be able to keep the mythic archetypes, the patterns of iterative imagery, the psychological motifs, clear and radiant in his mind. Jane Austen might turn *realist* on him, as she had on so many other readers, with consequences all too evident in the literature about her.

In Morris Zapp's view, the root of all critical error was a naïve confusion of literature with life. Life was transparent, literature opaque. Life was an open, literature a closed system. Life was composed of things, literature of words. Life was what it appeared to be about: if you were afraid your plane would crash it was about death, if you were trying to get a girl into bed it was about sex. Literature was never about what it appeared to be about, though in the case of the novel considerable ingenuity and perception were needed to crack the code of realistic illusion, which was why he had been professionally attracted to the genre (even the dumbest critic understood that *Hamlet* wasn't about how the guy could kill his uncle, or the *Ancient Mariner* about cruelty to animals, but it was surprising how many people thought that Jane Austen's novels were about finding Mr Right). The failure to keep the categories of life and literature distinct led to all kinds of heresy and nonsense: to 'liking' and 'not liking' books for instance, preferring some authors to others and suchlike whimsicalities which, he had constantly to remind his students, were of no conceivable interest to anyone except themselves (sometimes he shocked them by declaring that, speaking personally on this low, subjective level, he found Jane Austen a pain in the ass). He felt a particularly pressing need to castigate naïve theories of realism because they threatened his masterwork: obviously, if you applied an open-ended system (life) to a closed one (literature) the possible permutations were endless and the definitive commentary became an impossibility. Everything he knew about England warned him that the heresy flourished there with peculiar virulence, no doubt encouraged by the many concrete reminders of the actual historic existence of great authors that littered the country – baptismal registers, houses with plaques, second-best beds, reconstructed studies, engraved tombstones and suchlike trash. Well, one thing he was *not* going to do while he was in England was to visit Jane Austen's grave.

Textuality as Striptease

It is the spring of 1979, and Philip Swallow is now Professor and Head of the Department of English at Rummidge, which is hosting the annual conference of University Teachers of English. Morris Zapp has accepted his invitation to attend and give a lecture. Before the session (chaired by a senior member of the Department, Rupert Sutcliffe) Morris, who has embraced Deconstruction since the time of *Changing Places*, warns Philip that he is not going to like the lecture, entitled 'Textuality as Striptease'.

In the event, not many people did like Morris Zapp's lecture, and several members of the audience walked out before he had finished. Rupert Sutcliffe, obliged as chairman to sit facing the audience, assumed an aspect of glazed impassivity, but by imperceptible degrees the corners of his mouth turned down at more and more acute angles and his spectacles slid further and further down his nose as the discourse proceeded. Morris Zapp delivered it striding up and down the platform with his notes in one hand and a fat cigar in the other. 'You see before you,' he began, 'a man who once believed in the possibility of interpretation. That is, I thought that the goal of reading was to establish the meaning of texts. I used to be a Jane Austen man. I think I can say in all modesty I was *the* Jane Austen man. I wrote five books on Jane Austen, every one of which was trying to establish what her novels meant – and, naturally, to prove that no one had properly understood what they meant before. Then I began a commentary on the works of Jane Austen, the aim of which was to be utterly exhaustive, to examine the novels from every conceivable angle – historical, biographical, rhetorical, mythical, structural, Freudian, Jungian, Marxist, existentialist, Christian, allegorical, ethical, phenomenological, archetypal, you name it. So that when each commentary was written, there would be *nothing further to say* about the novel in question.

'Of course, I never finished it. The project was not so much Utopian as self-defeating. By that I don't just mean that if successful it would have eventually put us all out of business. I mean that it couldn't succeed because it isn't possible, and it isn't possible because of the nature of language itself, in which meaning is constantly being transferred from one signifier to another and can never be absolutely possessed.

'To understand a message is to decode it. Language is a code. *But every decoding is another encoding.* If you say something to me I check that I have understood your message by saying it back to you in my own words, that is, different words from the ones you used, for if I repeat your own words exactly you will doubt whether I have really understood you. But if I use *my* words it follows that I have changed *your* meaning, however slightly; and even if I were, deviantly, to indicate my comprehension by repeating back to you your own unaltered words, that is no guarantee that I have duplicated your meaning in my head, because I bring a different experience of language, literature, and non-verbal reality to those words, therefore they mean something different to me from what they mean to you. And if you think I have not understood the meaning of your message, you do not simply repeat it in the same words, you try to explain it in different words, different from the ones you used originally; but then the *it* is no longer the *it* that you started with. And for that matter, you are not the *you* that you started with. Time has moved on since you opened your mouth to speak, the molecules in your body have changed, what you intended to say has been superseded by what you did say, and that has already become part of your personal history, imperfectly remembered. Conversation is like playing tennis with a ball made of Krazy Putty that keeps coming back over the net in a different shape.

'Reading, of course, is different from conversation. It is more passive in the sense that we can't interact with the text, we can't affect the development of the text by our own words, since the text's words are already given. That is what perhaps encourages the quest for interpretation. If the words are fixed once and for all, on the page, may not their meaning be fixed also? Not so, because the same axiom, *every decoding is another encoding*, applies to literary criticism even more stringently than it does to ordinary spoken discourse. In ordinary spoken discourse, the endless cycle of encoding-decoding-encoding may be terminated by an action, as when for instance I say, "The door is open," and you say, "Do you mean you would like me to shut it?" and I say, "If you don't mind," and you shut the door – we may be satisfied that at a certain level my meaning has been understood. But if the literary text says, "The door was open," I cannot ask the text what it means by saying that the door was open, I can only speculate about the significance of that door – opened by what agency, leading to what discovery, mystery, goal? The tennis analogy will not do for the activity of reading – it is not a to-and-fro process, but an endless, tantalizing leading on, a flirtation without consummation, or if there is consummation, it is solitary, masturbatory. [Here the audience grew restive.] The reader plays with himself as the text plays upon him, plays upon his curiosity, desire, as a striptease dancer plays upon her audience's curiosity and desire.

'Now, as some of you know, I come from a city notorious for its bars and nightclubs featuring topless and bottomless dancers. I am told – I have not personally patronized these places, but I am told on the authority of no less a person than your host at this conference, my old friend Philip Swallow, who *has* patronized them, [here several members of the audience turned in their seats to stare and grin at Philip Swallow, who blushed to the roots of his silver-grey hair] that the girls take off all their clothes before they commence dancing in front of the customers. This is not striptease, it is all strip and no tease, it is the terpsichorean equivalent of the hermeneutic fallacy of a recuperable meaning, which claims that if we remove the clothing of its rhetoric from a literary text we discover the bare facts it is trying to communicate. The classical tradition of striptease, however, which goes back to Salome's dance of the seven veils and beyond, and which survives in a debased form in the dives of your Soho, offers a valid metaphor for the activity of reading. The dancer teases the audience, as the text teases its readers, with the promise of an ultimate revelation that is infinitely postponed. Veil after veil, garment after garment, is removed, but it is the *delay* in the stripping that makes it exciting, not the stripping itself; because no sooner has one secret been revealed than we lose interest in it and crave another. When we have seen the girl's underwear we want to see her body, when we have seen her breasts we want to see her buttocks, and when we have seen her buttocks we want to see her pubis, and when we see her pubis, the dance ends – but is our curiosity and desire satisfied? Of course not. The vagina remains hidden within the girl's body, shaded by her pubic hair, and even if she were to spread her legs before us [at this point several ladies in the audience noisily departed] it would still not satisfy the curiosity and desire set in motion by the stripping. Staring into that orifice we find that we have somehow overshot the goal of our quest, gone beyond pleasure in contemplated beauty; gazing into the womb we are returned to the mystery of our own origins. Just so in reading. The attempt to peer into the very core of a text, to possess once and for all its meaning, is vain – it is only ourselves that we find there, not the work itself. Freud said that obsessive reading (and I suppose that most of us in this room must be regarded as compulsive readers) – that obsessive reading is the displaced expression of a desire to see the mother's genitals [here a young man in the audience fainted and was carried out] but the point of the remark, which may not have been entirely appreciated by Freud himself, lies precisely in the concept of displacement. To read is to surrender oneself to an endless displacement of curiosity and desire from one sentence to another, from one action to another, from one level of the text to another. The text unveils itself before us, but never allows itself to be possessed; and instead of striving to possess it we should take pleasure in its teasing.'

Morris Zapp went on to illustrate his thesis with a number of passages from classic English and American literature. When he sat down, there was scattered and uneven applause.

'The floor is now open for discussion,' said Rupert Sutcliffe, surveying the audience apprehensively over the rims of his glasses. 'Are there any questions or comments?'

There was a long silence. Then Philip Swallow stood up. 'I have listened to your paper with great interest, Morris,' he said. 'Great interest. Your mind has lost none of its sharpness since we first met. But I am sorry to see that in the intervening years you have succumbed to the virus of structuralism.'

'I wouldn't call myself a structuralist,' Morris Zapp interrupted. 'A post-structuralist, perhaps.'

Philip Swallow made a gesture implying impatience with such subtle distinctions. 'I refer to that fundamental scepticism about the possibility of achieving certainty about anything, which I associate with the mischievous influence of Continental theorizing. There was a time when reading was a comparatively simple matter, something you learned to do in primary school. Now it seems to be some kind of arcane mystery, into which only a small élite have been initiated. I have been reading books for their meaning all my life – or at least that is what I have always thought I was doing. Apparently I was mistaken.'

'You weren't mistaken about what you were trying to do,' said Morris Zapp, relighting his cigar, 'you were mistaken in trying to do it.'

'I have just one question,' said Philip Swallow. 'It is this: what, with the greatest respect, is the point of our discussing your paper if, according to your own theory, we should not be discussing what you actually *said* at all, but discussing some imperfect memory or subjective interpretation of what you said?'

'There is no point,' said Morris Zapp blithely. 'If by point you mean the hope of arriving at some certain truth. But when did you ever discover *that* in a question-and-discussion session? Be honest, have you ever been to a lecture or seminar at the end of which you could have found two people present who could agree on the simplest précis of what had been said?'

'Then what in God's name *is* the point of it all?' cried Philip Swallow, throwing his hands into the air.

'The point, of course, is to uphold the institution of academic literary studies. We maintain our position in society by publicly performing a certain ritual, just like any other group of workers in the realm of discourse – lawyers, politicians, journalists. And as it looks as if we have done our duty for today, shall we all adjourn for a drink?'

'Tea, I'm afraid it will have to be,' said Rupert Sutcliffe, clutching with relief this invitation to bring the proceedings to a speedy close. 'Thank you *very* much for a most, er, stimulating and, ah, suggestive lecture.'

wheeeeeeeeeeeeeeeeeeeEEEEEEEEEEEEEE!

This evocation of the world of international academic conferences requires no introduction. Younger readers however may need one explanatory note: in the 1970s there was a notoriously sexist advertising campaign by an American airline which featured attractive air hostesses saying: '*Hi! I'm Julie* [or Donna, or Suzy, or Carol]. *Fly me!*'

whhhhheeeeeeeeeeeeEEEEEEEEEEEEEEEEEEEEEEEEEEEE!
To some people, there is no noise on earth as exciting as the sound of three or four big fan-jet engines rising in pitch, as the plane they are sitting in swivels at the end of the runway and, straining against its brakes, prepares for takeoff. The very danger in the situation is inseparable from the exhilaration it yields. You are strapped into your seat now, there is no way back, you have delivered yourself into the power of modern technology. You might as well lie back and enjoy it. *Whhheeeeeeeeeeeeeee!* And away we go, the acceleration like a punch in the small of the back, the grass glimpsed through the window flying backwards in a blur, and then falling out of sight suddenly as we soar into the sky. The plane banks to give us one last glimpse of home, flat and banal, before we break through the cloud cover and into the sunshine, the no-smoking sign goes

off with a ping, and a faint clink of bottles from the galley heralds the serving of cocktails. *Whheeeeeeeee!* Europe, here we come! Or Asia, or America, or wherever. It's June, and the conference season is well and truly open. In Oxford and Rummidge, to be sure, the students still sit at their desks in the examination halls, like prisoners in the stocks, but their teachers are able to flit off for a few days before the scripts come in for marking; while in North America the second semester of the academic year is already finished, papers have been graded, credits awarded, and the faculty are free to collect their travel grants and head east, or west, or wherever their fancy takes them. *Wheeeeeeeeee!*

The whole academic world seems to be on the move. Half the passengers on transatlantic flights these days are university teachers. Their luggage is heavier than average, weighed down with books and papers – and bulkier, because their wardrobes must embrace both formal wear and leisurewear, clothes for attending lectures in, and clothes for going to the beach in, or to the Museum, or the Schloss, or the Duomo, or the Folk Village. For that's the attraction of the conference circuit: it's a way of converting work into play, combining professionalism with tourism, and all at someone else's expense. Write a paper and see the world! I'm Jane Austen – fly me! Or Shakespeare, or T. S. Eliot, or Hazlitt. All tickets to ride, to ride the jumbo jets. *Wheeeeeeeeee!*

The air is thick with the babble of these wandering scholars' voices, their questions, complaints, advice, anecdotes. Which airline did you fly? How many stars does the hotel have? Why isn't the conference hall air-conditioned? Don't eat the salad here, they use human manure on the lettuce. Laker is cheap, but their terminal at LA is the pits. Swissair has excellent food. Cathay Pacific give you free drinks in economy. Pan Am are lousy timekeepers, though not as bad as Jugoslavian Airlines (its acronym JAT stands for 'joke about time'). Qantas has the best safety record among the international airlines, and Colombia the worst – one flight in three never arrives at its destination (OK, a slight exaggeration). On every El Al flight there are three secret servicemen with guns concealed in their briefcases, trained to shoot hijackers on sight – when taking something from your inside pocket, do it slowly and smile. Did you hear about the Irishman who tried to hijack a plane to Dublin? It was already going there. *Wheeeeeeeeeeeeeee!*

Hijackings are only one of the hazards of modern travel. Every summer there is some kind of disruption of the international airways – a strike of French air-traffic controllers, a go-slow by British baggage handlers, a war in the Middle East. This year it's the worldwide grounding of the DC-10, following a crash at Chicago's O'Hare Airport on May 25th, when one of these planes shed an engine on takeoff and plunged to the ground, killing everyone on board. The captain's last recorded word was 'Damn.' Stronger expletives are used by travellers fighting at the counters of travel agencies to transfer their tickets to airlines operating Boeing 747s and Lockheed Tristars; or at having to accept a seat on some slow, clapped-out DC-8 with no movies and blocked toilets, flying to Europe via Newfoundland and Reykjavik. Many conferees arrive

at their destinations this summer more than usually
fatigued, dehydrated and harassed; the dying fall of the
engines' *WHHHEEEEEEEeeeeeeeee*, as the power is finally
switched off, is sweet music to their ears, but their chat-
ter is undiminished, their demand for information
insatiable.

How much should you tip? What's the best way to
get downtown from the airport? Can you understand
the menu? Tip taxis ten per cent in Bangladesh, five
per cent in Italy; in Mexico it is not necessary, and in
Japan the driver will be positively insulted if you do.
Narita airport is forty kilometres from downtown
Tokyo. There is a fast electric train, but it stops short
of the city centre – best take the limousine bus. The
Greek word for bus stop is *stasis*. The Polish word for
scrambled eggs is *jajecznice*, pronounced 'yighyehch-
neetseh', which is sort of onomatopoeic, if you can
get your tongue round it. In Israel, breakfast eggs are
served soft-boiled and cold – yuk. In Korea, they eat
soup at breakfast. Also at lunch and dinner. In Norway
they have dinner at four o'clock in the afternoon, in
Spain at ten o'clock at night. In Tokyo the nightclubs
close at 11.30 p.m., in Berlin they are only just beginning to open by then.

Oh, the amazing variety of *langue* and *parole*, food
and custom, in the countries of the world! But almost
equally amazing is the way a shared academic interest
will overcome these differences. All over the world, in
hotels, university residences and conference centres, in
châteaux and villas and country houses, in capital cities
and resort towns, beside lakes, among mountains, on

the shores of seas cold and warm, people of every colour and nation are gathered together to discuss the novels of Thomas Hardy, or the problem plays of Shakespeare, or the postmodernist short story, or the poetics of Imagism. And, of course, not all the conferences that are going on this summer are concerned with English literature, not by any means. There are at the same time conferences in session on French medieval *chansons* and Spanish poetic drama of the sixteenth century and the German *Sturm und Drang* movement and Serbian folk-songs; there are conferences on the dynasties of ancient Crete and the social history of the Scottish Highlands and the foreign policy of Bismarck and the sociology of sport and the economic controversy over monetarism; there are conferences on low-temperature physics and microbiology and oral pathology and quasars and catastrophe theory. Sometimes, when two conferences share the same accommodation, confusions occur: it has been known for a bibliographer specializing in the history of punctuation to sit through the first twenty minutes of a medical paper on 'Malfunctions of the Colon' before he realized his mistake.

But, on the whole, academic subject groups are self-defining, exclusive entities. Each has its own jargon, pecking order, newsletter, professional association. The members probably meet only once a year – at a conference. Then, what a lot of hallos, howareyous, and whatareyouworkingons, over the drinks, over the meals, between lectures. Let's have a drink, let's have dinner, let's have breakfast together. It's this kind of informal contact, of course, that's the real *raison d'être* of a conference, not the programme of papers and lectures which has ostensibly brought the participants together, but which most of them find intolerably tedious.

Just a Cigarette

In *Nice Work*, Robyn Penrose, a young lecturer in English
Literature at Rummidge University, committed to feminism
and literary theory, is required to 'shadow' Vic Wilcox,
Managing Director of a local foundry and engineering
firm, as part of an Industry Year initiative to improve
relations between academia and industry.

Pringle's was definitely a business dealing in real
commodities and running it was not in the least like
doing literary theory, but it did strike Robyn sometimes
that Vic Wilcox stood to his subordinates in the relation
of teacher to pupils. Though she could seldom grasp
the detailed matters of engineering and accounting that
he dealt with in his meetings with his staff, though these
meetings often bored and wearied her, she could see
that he was trying to *teach* the other men, to coax and
persuade them to look at the factory's operations in a
new way. He would have been surprised to be told it,
but he used the Socratic method: he prompted the other
directors and the middle managers and even the fore-
men to identify the problems themselves and to reach
by their own reasoning the solutions he had himself
already determined upon. It was so deftly done that she
had sometimes to temper her admiration by reminding

herself that it was all directed by the profit-motive, and that beyond the walls of Vic Wilcox's carpeted office there was a factory full of men and women doing dangerous, demeaning and drearily repetitive tasks, who were mere cogs in the machine of his grand strategy. He was an artful tyrant, but still a tyrant. Furthermore, he showed no reciprocal respect for her own professional skills.

A typical instance of this was the furious argument they had about the Silk Cut advertisement. They were returning in his car from visiting a foundry in Derby that had been taken over by asset-strippers who were selling off an automatic core moulder Wilcox was interested in, though it had turned out to be too old-fashioned for his purpose. Every few miles, it seemed, they passed the same huge poster on roadside hoardings, a photographic depiction of a rippling expanse of purple silk in which there was a single slit, as if the material had been slashed with a razor. There were no words on the advertisement, except for the Government Health Warning about smoking. This ubiquitous image, flashing past at regular intervals, both irritated and intrigued Robyn, and she began to do her semiotic stuff on the deep structure hidden beneath its bland surface.

It was in the first instance a kind of riddle. That is to say, in order to decode it, you had to know that there was a brand of cigarettes called Silk Cut. The poster was the iconic representation of a missing name, like a rebus. But the icon was also a metaphor. The shimmering silk, with its voluptuous curves and sensuous texture, obviously symbolized the female body, and the elliptical slit, foregrounded by a lighter colour showing through, was still more obviously a vagina. The advert thus appealed to both sensual and sadistic impulses, the desire to mutilate as well as penetrate the female body.

Vic Wilcox spluttered with outraged derision as she expounded this interpretation. He smoked a different brand, himself, but it was as if he felt his whole philosophy of life was threatened by Robyn's analysis of the advert. 'You must have a twisted mind to see all that in a perfectly harmless bit of cloth,' he said.

'What's the point of it, then?' Robyn challenged him. 'Why use cloth to advertise cigarettes?'

'Well, that's the name of 'em, isn't it? Silk Cut. It's a picture of the name. Nothing more or less.'

'Suppose they'd used a picture of a roll of silk cut in half – would that do just as well?'

'I suppose so. Yes, why not?'

'Because it would look like a penis cut in half, that's why.'

He forced a laugh to cover his embarrassment. 'Why can't you people take things at their face value?'

'What people are you referring to?'

'Highbrows. Intellectuals. You're always trying to find hidden meanings in things. Why? A cigarette is a cigarette. A piece of silk is a piece of silk. Why not leave it at that?'

'When they're represented they acquire additional meanings,' said Robyn. 'Signs are never innocent. Semiotics teaches us that.'

'Semi-what?'

'Semiotics. The study of signs.'

'It teaches us to have dirty minds, if you ask me.'

'Why d'you think the wretched cigarettes were called Silk Cut in the first place?'

'I dunno. It's just a name, as good as any other.'

'"Cut" has something to do with the tobacco, doesn't it? The way the tobacco leaf is cut. Like "Player's Navy Cut" – my uncle Walter used to smoke them.'

'Well, what if it does?' Vic said warily.

'But silk has nothing to do with tobacco. It's a metaphor, a metaphor that means something like, "smooth as silk". Somebody in an advertising agency dreamt up the name "Silk Cut" to suggest a cigarette that wouldn't give you a sore throat or a hacking cough or lung cancer. But after a while the public got used to the name, the word "Silk" ceased to signify, so they decided to have an advertising campaign to give the brand a high profile again. Some bright spark in the agency came up with the idea of rippling silk with a cut in it. The original metaphor is now represented literally. But new metaphorical connotations accrue – sexual ones. Whether they were consciously intended or not doesn't really matter. It's a good example of the perpetual sliding of the signified under the signifier, actually.'

Wilcox chewed on this for a while, then said, 'Why do women smoke them, then, eh?' His triumphant expression showed that he thought this was a knockdown argument. 'If smoking Silk Cut is a form of aggravated rape, as you try to make out, how come women smoke 'em too?'

'Many women are masochistic by temperament,' said

Robyn. 'They've learned what's expected of them in a patriarchal society.'

'Ha!' Wilcox exclaimed, tossing back his head. 'I might have known you'd have some daft answer.'

'I don't know why you're so worked up,' said Robyn. 'It's not as if you smoke Silk Cut yourself.'

'No, I smoke Marlboros. Funnily enough, I smoke them because I like the taste.'

'They're the ones that have the lone cowboy ads, aren't they?'

'I suppose that makes me a repressed homosexual, does it?'

'No, it's a very straightforward metonymic message.'

'Metowhat?'

'Metonymic. One of the fundamental tools of semiotics is the distinction between metaphor and metonymy. D'you want me to explain it to you?'

'It'll pass the time,' he said.

'Metaphor is a figure of speech based on similarity, whereas metonymy is based on contiguity. In metaphor you substitute something *like* the thing you mean for the thing itself, whereas in metonymy you substitute some attribute or cause or effect of the thing for the thing itself.'

'I don't understand a word you're saying.'

'Well, take one of your moulds. The bottom bit is called the drag because it's dragged across the floor and the top bit is called the cope because it covers the bottom bit.'

'I told *you* that.'

'Yes, I know. What you didn't tell me was that "drag" is a metonymy and "cope" is a metaphor.'

Vic grunted. 'What difference does it make?'

'It's just a question of understanding how language works. I thought you were interested in how things work.'

'I don't see what it's got to do with cigarettes.'

'In the case of the Silk Cut poster, the picture signifies the female body metaphorically: the slit in the silk is *like* a vagina –'

Vic flinched at the word. 'So you say.'

'All holes, hollow spaces, fissures and folds represent the female genitals.'

'Prove it.'

'Freud proved it, by his successful analysis of dreams,' said Robyn. 'But the Marlboro ads don't use any metaphors. That's probably why you smoke them, actually.'

'What d'you mean?' he said suspiciously.

'You don't have any sympathy with the metaphorical way of looking at things. A cigarette is a cigarette as far as you are concerned.'

'Right.'

'The Marlboro ad doesn't disturb that naïve faith in the stability of the signified. It establishes a metonymic connection – completely spurious of course, but realistically plausible – between smoking that particular brand and the healthy, heroic, outdoor life of the cowboy. Buy the cigarette and you buy the life-style, or the fantasy of living it.'

'Rubbish!' said Wilcox. 'I hate the country and the open air. I'm scared to go into a field with a cow in it.'

'Well then, maybe it's the solitariness of the cowboy in the ads that appeals to you. Self-reliant, independent, very macho.'

'I've never heard such a lot of balls in all my life,' said Vic Wilcox, which was strong language coming from him.

'Balls – now that's an interesting expression . . .' Robyn mused.

'Oh no!' he groaned.

'When you say a man "has balls", approvingly, it's a metonymy, whereas if you say something is a "lot of balls", or "a balls-up", it's a sort of metaphor. The metonymy attributes value to the testicles whereas the metaphor uses them to degrade something else.'

'I can't take any more of this,' said Vic. 'D'you mind if I smoke? Just a plain, ordinary cigarette?'

'If I can have Radio Three on,' said Robyn.

A Tutorial

Vic Wilcox becomes infatuated with Robyn Penrose, much
to her embarrassment and annoyance, and after the
termination of the Shadow Scheme he pesters her with
messages which she leaves unanswered. One day he turns
up at the University, having persuaded the Vice Chancellor
that it would be a good idea to continue the scheme in
reverse, with himself sitting in on Robyn's classes. Robyn,
whose job is insecure, is obliged to agree through gritted
teeth. Her student, Marion Russell, who is due to present
that morning's tutorial essay, has encountered Vic before,
when moonlighting as a Kissogram girl.

Robyn led Vic Wilcox along the corridor to her room.

'I consider this an underhand trick,' she said, when
they were alone.

'What d'you mean?'

'You're not trying to pretend, are you, that you're
genuinely interested in finding out how University
Departments of English operate?'

'Yes I am, I'm very interested.' He looked round the
room. 'Have you read all these books?'

'When I first came to Pringle's, you expressed utter
contempt for the kind of work I do.'

'I was prejudiced,' he said. 'That's what this Shadow

Scheme is all about, overcoming prejudice.'

'I think you fixed this up as an excuse to see me,' said Robyn. She hoicked her Gladstone bag on to the desk and began to unpack books, folders, essays.

'I want to see what you do,' said Vic. 'I'm willing to learn. I've been reading those books you mentioned, *Jane Eyre* and *Wuthering Heights*.'

Robyn could not resist the bait. 'And what did you think of them?'

'*Jane Eyre* was all right. A bit long-winded. With *Wuthering Heights* I kept getting in a muddle about who was who.'

'That's deliberate, of course,' said Robyn.

'Is it?'

'The same names keep cropping up in different permutations and different generations. Cathy the older is born Catherine Earnshaw and becomes Catherine Linton by marriage. Cathy the younger is born Catherine Linton, becomes Catherine Heathcliff by her first marriage to Linton Heathcliff, the son of Isabella Linton and Heathcliff, and later becomes Catherine Earnshaw by her second marriage to Hareton Earnshaw, so she ends up with the same name as her mother, Catherine Earnshaw.'

'You should go on "Mastermind",' said Vic.

'It's incredibly confusing, especially with all the time-shifts as well,' said Robyn. 'It's what makes *Wuthering Heights* such a remarkable novel for its period.'

'I don't see the point. More people would enjoy it if it was more straightforward.'

'Difficulty generates meaning. It makes the reader work harder.'

'But reading is the opposite of work,' said Vic. 'It's what you do when you come home from work, to relax.'

'In this place,' said Robyn, 'reading is work. Reading is production. And what we produce is meaning.'

There was a knock on the door, which slowly opened to the extent of about eighteen inches. The head of Marion Russell appeared around the edge of the door like a glove puppet, goggled at Robyn and Vic, and withdrew. The door closed again, and whispering and scuffling on the other side of it were faintly audible, like the sounds of mice.

'That's my ten o'clock tutorial,' said Robyn.

'Is ten o'clock when you usually start work?'

'I never stop working,' said Robyn. 'If I'm not working here, I'm working at home. This isn't a factory, you know. We don't clock in and out. Sit in that corner and make yourself as inconspicuous as possible.'

'What's this tutorial about, then?'

'Tennyson. Here, take this.' She gave him a copy of Tennyson's *Poems*, a cheap Victorian edition with sentimental illustrations that she had bought from a second-hand bookshop as a student and used for years, until Ricks' Longman's Annotated edition was published. She went to the door and opened it. 'Right, come in,' she said, smiling encouragingly.

It was Marion Russell's turn to start off the tutorial discussion, by reading a short paper on a topic she had chosen herself from an old exam paper; but when the students filed into the room and seated themselves round the table, she was missing.

'Where's Marion?' Robyn asked.

'She's gone to the cloakroom,' said Laura Jones, a big girl in a navy-blue track suit, who was doing Joint Honours in English and Physical Education, and was a champion shot putter.

'She said she didn't feel well,' said Helen Lorimer, whose nails were painted with green nail-varnish to match her hair, and who wore plastic earrings depicting a smiling face on one ear and a frowning face on the other.

'She gave me her essay to read out,' said Simon Bradford, a thin, eager young man, with thick-lensed spectacles and wispy beard.

'Wait a minute,' said Robyn, 'I'll go and see what's the matter with her. Oh, by the way – this is Mr Wilcox, he's observing this class as part of an Industry Year project. I suppose you all know this is Industry Year, don't you?' They looked blankly at her. 'Ask Mr Wilcox to explain it to you,' she said, as she left the room.

She found Marion Russell hiding in the staff women's lavatory. 'What's the matter, Marion?' she said briskly. 'Pre-menstrual tension?'

'That man,' said Marion Russell. 'He was the one at the factory, wasn't he?'

'Yes.'

'What's he doing here? Has he come to complain?'

'No, of course not. He's here to observe the tutorial.'

'What for?'

'It's too complicated to explain now. Come along, we're all waiting for you.'

'I can't.'

'Why not?'

'It's too embarrassing. He's seen me in my knickers and stuff.'

'He won't recognize you.'

''Course he will.'

'No he won't. You look entirely different.' Marion Russell was wearing harem pants and an outsize T-shirt with Bob Geldof's face imprinted on it like the face of Christ on Veronica's napkin.

'What did you do your paper on?'

'The struggle between optimism and pessimism in Tennyson's verse,' said Marion Russell.

'Come on, then, let's hear it.'

If Vic had been explaining Industry Year to the other three students, he had been very brief, for the room was silent when Robyn returned with Marion Russell. Vic was frowning at his copy of Tennyson, and the students were watching him as rabbits watch a stoat. He looked up as Marion came in, but, as Robyn had predicted, his eyes signalled no flicker of recognition.

Marion began reading her paper in a low monotone. All went well until she observed that the line from 'Locksley Hall', *'Let the great world spin for ever, down the ringing grooves of change'*, reflected the confidence of the Victorian Railway Age. Vic raised his hand.

'Yes, Mr Wilcox?' Robyn's tone and regard were as discouraging as she could make them.

'He must have been thinking of trams, not trains,' said Vic. 'Train wheels don't run in grooves.'

Simon Bradford gave an abrupt, high-pitched laugh;

then, on meeting Robyn's eye, looked as if he wished he hadn't.

'D'you find that suggestion amusing, Simon?' she said.

'Well,' he said, 'trams. They're not very poetic, are they?'

'It said the Railway Age in this book I read,' said Marion.

'What book, Marion?' asked Robyn.

'Some critical book. I can't remember which one, now,' said Marion, riffling randomly through a sheaf of notes.

'Always acknowledge secondary sources,' said Robyn. 'Actually, it's quite an interesting, if trivial, point. When he wrote the poem, Tennyson was under the impression that railway trains ran in grooves.' She read out the footnote from her Longman's Annotated edition: '"*When I went by the first train from Liverpool to Manchester in 1830 I thought that the wheels ran in a groove. It was a black night, and there was such a vast crowd round the train at the station that we could not see the wheels. Then I made this line."*'

It was Vic's turn to laugh. 'Well, he didn't make it very well, did he?'

'So, what's the answer?' said Laura, a rather literal-minded girl who wrote down everything Robyn said in tutorials. 'Is it a train or a tram?'

'Both or either,' said Robyn. 'It doesn't really matter. Go on, Marion.'

'Hang about,' said Vic. 'You can't have it both ways. "*Grooves*" is a whadyoucallit, metonymy, right?'

The students were visibly impressed as he brought

out this technical term. Robyn herself was rather touched that he had remembered it, and it was almost with regret that she corrected him.

'No,' said Robyn. 'It's a metaphor. *"The grooves of change"* is a metaphor. The world moving through time is compared to something moving along a metal track.'

'But the grooves tell you what kind of track.'

'True,' Robyn conceded. 'It's metonymy inside a metaphor. Or to be precise, a synecdoche: part for whole.'

'But if I have a picture of grooves in my head, I can't think of a train. It has to be a tram.'

'What do the rest of you think?' said Robyn. 'Helen?'

Helen Lorimer reluctantly raised her eyes to meet Robyn's. 'Well, if Tennyson thought he was describing a train, then it's a train, I s'pose,' she said.

'Not necessarily,' said Simon Bradford. 'That's the Intentional Fallacy.' He glanced at Robyn for approval. Simon Bradford had attended one of her seminars in Critical Theory the previous year. Helen Lorimer, who hadn't, and who had plainly never heard of the Intentional Fallacy, looked despondent, like the earring on her left ear.

There was a brief silence, during which all looked expectantly at Robyn.

'It's an aporia,' said Robyn. 'A kind of accidental aporia, a figure of undecidable ambiguity, irresolvable contradiction. We know Tennyson intended an allusion to railways, and, as Helen said, we can't erase that knowledge.' (At this flattering paraphrase of her argument,

Helen Lorimer's expression brightened, resembling her right earring.) 'But we also know that railway trains don't run in grooves, and nothing that *does* run in grooves seems metaphorically adequate to the theme. As Simon said, trams aren't very poetic. So the reader's mind is continually baffled in its efforts to make sense of the line.'

'You mean, it's a duff line?' said Vic.

'On the contrary,' said Robyn, 'I think it's one of the few good ones in the poem.'

'If there's a question about the Railway Age in Finals,' said Laura Jones, 'can we quote it?'

'Yes, Laura,' said Robyn patiently. 'As long as you show you're aware of the aporia.'

'How d'you spell that?'

Robyn wrote the word with a coloured felt-tip on the whiteboard screwed to the wall of her office. '*Aporia*. In classical rhetoric it means real or pretended uncertainty about the subject under discussion. Deconstructionists today use it to refer to more radical kinds of contradiction or subversion of logic or defeat of the reader's expectation in a text. You could say that it's deconstruction's favourite trope. Hillis Miller compares it to following a mountain path and then finding that it gives out, leaving you stranded on a ledge, unable to go back or forwards. It actually derives from a Greek word meaning "a pathless path". Go on, Marion.'

A few minutes later, Vic, evidently encouraged by the success of his intervention over '*grooves*', put up his hand again. Marion had been arguing, reasonably enough, that Tennyson was stronger on emotions than on ideas, and had quoted in support the lyrical outburst of the lover in 'Maud', *'Come into the garden, Maud, /For the black bat night has flown.'*

'Yes, Mr Wilcox?' said Robyn, frowning.

'That's a song,' said Vic. '"Come into the garden, Maud". My grandad used to sing it.'

'Yes?'

'Well, the bloke in the poem is singing a song to his girl, a well-known song. It makes a difference, doesn't it?'

'Tennyson wrote "Come into the garden, Maud", as a poem,' said Robyn. 'Somebody else set it to music later.'

'Oh,' said Vic. 'My mistake. Or is it an aporia?'

'No, it's a mistake,' said Robyn. 'I must ask you not to interrupt any more, please, or Marion will never finish her paper.'

Vic lapsed into a hurt silence. He stirred restlessly in his seat, he sighed impatiently to himself from time to time in a way that made the students stall nervously in the middle of what they were saying, he licked his fingers to turn the pages of his book, and flexed it so violently in his hands that the spine cracked noisily, but he didn't actually interrupt again. After a while he seemed to lose interest in the discussion and to be browsing in the Tennyson on his own account. When the tutorial was over and the students had left, he asked Robyn if he could borrow it.

'Of course. Why, though?'

'Well, I thought if I have a read of it, I might have a better idea of what's going on next week.'

'Oh, but we're not doing Tennyson next week. It's *Daniel Deronda*, I think.'

'You mean, you've finished with Tennyson? That's it?'

'As far as this group is concerned, yes.'

'But you never told them whether he was optimistic or pessimistic.'

'I don't tell them what to think,' said Robyn.

'Then how are they supposed to learn the right answers?'

'There are no right answers to questions like that. There are only interpretations.'

'What's the point of it, then?' he said. 'What's the point of sitting around discussing books all day, if you're no wiser at the end of it?'

'Oh, you're *wiser*,' said Robyn. 'What you learn is that language is an infinitely more devious and slippery medium than you had supposed.'

'That's good for you?'

'Very good for you,' she said, tidying the books and papers on her desk. 'Do you want to borrow *Daniel Deronda* for next week?'

'What did he write?'

'He's not a he, he's a book. By George Eliot.'

'Good writer, is he, this Eliot bloke?'

'He was a she, actually. You see how slippery language is. But, yes, very good. D'you want to swap *Daniel Deronda* for the Tennyson?'

'I'll take them both,' he said. 'There's some good stuff in here.' He opened the Tennyson, and read aloud, tracing the lines with his blunt forefinger:

'Woman is the lesser man, and all thy passions,
    matched with mine,
Are as moonlight unto sunlight, and as water
    unto wine.'

'I might have guessed you would lap up "Locksley Hall",' said Robyn.

'It strikes a chord,' he said, turning the pages. 'Why didn't you answer my letters?'

'Because I didn't read them,' she said. 'I didn't even open them.'

'That wasn't very nice.'

'I knew all too well what would be in them,' she said. 'And if you're going to get stupid and sentimental, and sick Tennyson all over me, I'm going to call off The Shadow Scheme Part Two right away.'

POCKET PENGUINS